PLAYS FOR PERFORMANCE

———————————

*A series designed for
contemporary production and study
Edited by
Nicholas Rudall and Bernard Sahlins*

EURIPIDES

Medea

In a New Translation by
Nicholas Rudall

Ivan R. Dee
CHICAGO

Library of Congress Cataloging-in-Publication Data:
Euripides.
   [Medea. English]
   Medea / Eruipides ; in a new translation by Nicholas Rudall.
      p. cm. — (Plays for performance)
   ISBN 1-56663-320-6 (cloth : alk. paper) — ISBN 1-56663-321-4 (pbk. : alk. paper)
    1. Medea (Greek mythology) — Drama. I. Rudall, Nicholas. II. Title. III. Series.
PA3975.M4R83 2000
882'.01—dc21   00-040506

INTRODUCTION

by Nicholas Rudall

The *Medea* of Euripides has haunted the stages of Western theatre, in translations, adaptations, and operatic reincarnations, for 2,400 years. There *was* a myth, many myths that told the story of Jason and Medea. But it was Euripides' particular genius that gave the story shape and emotional complexity. Infanticide is his subject. And that in itself makes the horrified voyeur in us want to look and try to understand.

The play was performed in 431 B.C. Athens was already at war with its fellow Greeks. Some twenty years later, after Athens had decimated the island of Melos, enslaved and raped its women, and killed all its men, Euripides wrote *The Trojan Women*. He catalogued the atrocities of "civilized" Greeks against "barbarian" women. The *Medea* is the disturbing precursor of this later but utter condemnation.

This, I think, is how a modern production must begin its search. The *Medea* can too easily fall into melodrama if some fundamental Greek concepts are ignored. Yes, Medea is a barbarian. Yes, she is, literally, a witch with superhuman powers. Yes, she ultimately kills her own children. But there is a history which more than partially provides her with justification for her acts. The history is this: she saved Jason by destroying her own family; she saved Jason by making the daughters of Pelias kill their own family. And

3

now she is here in Corinth and her own family is about to be destroyed.

There is no true modern word that expresses the Greek word *oikos*. *Oikos* means house and home and family. In the yet struggling Greek conceptions of Justice, the Mediterranean idea of "an eye for an eye" prevailed. Given that structure, Medea has lost or destroyed two *oikoi* in order to save Jason. Now he has destroyed hers. He has remarried and abandoned their children. In her eyes, and indeed in the eyes of some of those who watched this play, her decision to destroy his *oikos* was a natural balance.

What makes the play sublime is that her revenge is complete and in its completeness, tragic. She not only kills the new family but the old. Yet she loves the old far more than Jason. In order to achieve her sense of Justice, of balance, of total reciprocity, she must destroy his *oikos*. Yet she loves his *oikos* far more than he. Despite the pity we feel for Jason at the end of this play, it is Medea who has lost, Medea whose pain is deepest, Medea whose loved dead children she holds in her arms.

In a sense Medea, while behaving like a barbarian, has used the rhetoric and the ethical constructs of the civilized Greek world to justify her horrifying revenge. Euripides has made her case initially plausible by his characterizations of Creon and Jason. Creon is an atypical tyrant. He blusters but has no resolve. He is a man with no real concern for her plight, and Medea is able to outwit him in almost an instant. Jason is a Greek hero, a civilized intellectual whose rhetoric is self-serving and merely opportune.

In the first two-thirds of the play our sympathies lie heavily with Medea. But once the rigor of her argument begins to take hold we, like the chorus of her female friends, begin to beg her to change her mind. Although there is a perfection of balance in her revenge, although Jason is a specious hero, infanticide is too horrible. But even when our sympathies are being questioned, Euripides gives us scenes in which Medea's love for her children can break an audience's heart. He was a master of pathos. When she weeps and kisses her children, lingers longingly in thinking of what might have been, we know that she loves them, know that when she kills them she will lose far more than Jason. Although we feel an unexpected surge of pity for Jason, desolate and alone, in the end it is Medea's tragedy.

Like all the other plays in this series, this translation was made with performance in mind. It is written to be spoken, and, if a director chooses to make such use of the choral odes, occasionally to be sung. It aims at clarity and simplicity (the original Greek is predominantly conversational). I tried to find the short staccato of modern English where Greek syntax is elongated and filled with subordinate clauses. I hope that this still retains a distinct feeling of an elevated style—but devoid of archaisms and free from colloquialisms.

I have also tried to give individual characters specific speech patterns (as Euripides surely did). Medea is quick, deeply ironic, occasionally morbidly funny, and capable of passions ranging from seething anger to weeping regret. Jason is a politician. He speaks well and lies—perhaps believing that he speaks the truth. I have attempted to translate what was, of course, contemporary Greek for its first audience into contemporary English for a modern audience.

CHARACTERS

MEDEA
NURSE
TUTOR to Medea's sons
CHORUS of Corinthian women
CREON, king of Corinth
JASON, Medea's husband
AEGEUS, king of Athens
MESSENGER
TWO CHILDREN of Medea

Medea

NURSE: I wish they had never set sail! I wish the *Argo* had never passed through the straits where the grey rocks loom—and then made its way to Colchis. I wish the pine tree on Mount Pelion had never felt the axe, had never fallen to the ground. For then the heroes, the Argonauts, would never have put oars in their hands. They would never have heard the command of King Pelias to bring home the Golden Fleece. Medea, my mistress would never have set sail for Iolchos. She was madly in love with Jason. And after the daughters of Pelias—yes Medea gave the command—killed their father, she would never have come here to Corinth to live with Jason and her children. She came here as an exile. But the people of Corinth have taken her into their hearts.

She is an obedient wife. And when a wife bends to her husband's will, that can save a marriage.

But now her world has turned to hate. She is wounded precisely where her love was deep.

Jason has betrayed her. He has abandoned his own sons, taken a new bride, Glauke, the daughter of Creon, king of Corinth.

Ah, Medea. I pity her. She is scorned, she is shamed. She has gone mad. She remembers every oath, every promise that Jason made to her. She lies on the ground in agony. She weeps. And time is drenched with her tears. Since the moment she heard of Jason's cruelty, she has not raised her eyes or her face from the ground. When her friends try to comfort her, she hears nothing. She might as well be a rock or a wave of the sea. Sometimes she turns that beautiful face away and speaks to herself alone. She moans aloud for her father, her country, her home. For she betrayed them all to come here with this man who now abandons her, insults her to her face.

Ah, Medea. I pity her.

Now she knows the pain of one who has left her homeland. Happiness is denied her. She hates her sons, hates even to see them. I am afraid she is planning something dreadful in that mind of hers. She is a woman who inspires terror. Make her your enemy and you'll not find an easy victory.

Ah, here come the boys, they've been out playing. They know nothing of the cruelty being inflicted on their mother. Well, they're young. And when you're young, you don't see the pain around you.

TUTOR: *(with Medea's children)* Nurse, what are you doing out here, standing by the door, all alone and talking to yourself? Trouble, trouble—that's all you talk about. You're supposed to be my mistress's servant. What does she say when you leave her all alone?

NURSE: Let me tell you—you're a good old friend, a fine tutor to the boys—a faithful slave feels in her heart the pain that wounds her mistress. It was all too much to keep in. I had to come out here to tell the earth and the sky how my mistress has been wronged.

TUTOR: Oh I pity her. Has she not stopped crying?

NURSE: Stopped crying? Don't be a fool. Her grief has only now seen the light of day—and it will grow.

TUTOR: *She's* the fool—though I shouldn't talk like that about my mistress. She had better save her tears. There's more to come, and it's worse.

NURSE: Worse? Tell me! What has happened?

TUTOR: Nothing. I'm sorry I opened my mouth.

NURSE: Look, you're a slave, I'm a slave. You can trust me. What's the news? I can hold my tongue.

TUTOR: I was down where the old men sit and play dice—next to the holy fountain of Peirene. I pretended I wasn't listening. But I heard one of the men say that Creon is going to send these boys away, banish them—their mother too. I don't know if it's true. I hope not.

NURSE: Jason won't allow his sons to be banished from Corinth. Surely not? Even if he has broken with their mother?

TUTOR: A new love lies in the bed of the old. Jason cares nothing for this family.

NURSE: Then it's all over. The suffering was hard enough before. *This* is the end.

TUTOR: Now listen—don't say a word to Medea. Keep quiet. Not a word—you understand?

NURSE: Children, do you know what kind of father you have? My curse upon—No—he is my master. But he is guilty. He has betrayed those who loved him.

TUTOR: Every man is guilty. You're old enough to know that every man loves himself more than his neighbor. Jason is in love. These boys mean nothing to him now.

NURSE: *(to the boys)* Off you go. Into the house now. Everything is going to be all right. *(to the Tutor)* Do all you can to keep them away from her. When her mood's as black as this, don't let them go near her. I've seen her watching them—her eyes like a wild bull. She's up to something. And I know she won't let her anger cool until she has struck her victim. But I pray to god she strikes her enemies, not her friends.

MEDEA: *(inside the palace)* Ah the pain, the agony! It is too much to bear. I want to die!

NURSE: There! Did you hear? It is your mother torturing her heart and whipping her anger. Quick, my little ones, go inside. Stay out of your mother's sight. Don't go near her. It's safer that way. When she is angry and has set her mind on something, she can be cruel and dangerous. Go on now, go inside. *(the children and the Tutor leave)* Her grief is beginning to swell like a large black cloud. Soon it will burst in a storm of fury. She has been scorned. Her passions run deep and will never be soothed. What will she do?

MEDEA: *(inside)* Oh I suffer, I suffer. Oh how have I been wronged! Should I not weep?
My children, your father hates me and you are doomed. Die die die! You and your father and all his house.

NURSE: Oh the sorrow—the pity. Oh Medea, why? Why your children? What have they done? Their father is the guilty one. Do not hate them.
Oh my children, I am sick with terror. I fear what may happen to you. Medea is of royal blood and her power is awesome. She does not obey commands, she gives them. Once her anger is aroused, she does not easily forget.
I am just an ordinary, common person. That suits me. I have no need for the grand life. Give me

peace and quiet as I grow old. Not too great, not too small. Somewhere in the middle. That's the best—and practice what you preach. To be rich and powerful does not bring happiness. And when the gods are angry the rich and the powerful have further to fall.

(enter Chorus of Corinthian women)

CHORUS: I heard her cry.
  Oh that poor woman from Colchis,
  I heard her cry.
  She does not know peace.
  Nurse, speak to us.
  As I stood by the door I heard her weeping deep in the palace.
  When Jason's household suffers, I suffer too.
  For I love this house.

NURSE: Jason's household? It is no more. It is gone.
  Jason is a prisoner in the bed of a princess.
  Medea is a prisoner in the tears that rob her of her life.
  You cannot comfort her.

MEDEA: *(inside)* Come! Let the lightning pierce my skull.
  What is there to live for now?
  I hate this cruel life.
  I want an end,
  An end to this pain
  An end to this life.

CHORUS: Oh Zeus, oh Earth, oh Light!
  Do you hear her prayers?
  The prayers of a wife in pain.

(to Medea who is still inside the palace)

This is madness—

To seek the fate that all men fear.
Oh do not pray for death.
If Jason has found new love,
It is common. Let it rest.
Zeus will never forsake you.
This grief,
This passion
Is eating at your heart.

MEDEA: Oh Themis, Great Artemis,
Do you see how I am treated?
Aaaagh! This man that I hate!
This man who swore eternity in my arms!
Let me live to see him and his bride as broken bod-
ies in the dust of their palace.
They have wronged me!
Never did I deserve this.
For Jason I left my father.
For Jason I left my home.
For Jason I killed my own brother—
To my shame, Zeus, to my shame.

NURSE: Do you hear? She calls on Themis, who gives
Justice to mankind.
She calls on Zeus, who protects the oaths that
human beings swear.
Her rage runs deep.
It will not end in peace.

CHORUS: I wish she would leave the palace.
I want to see her, talk to her.
Perhaps our words could bring her peace
And calm her rage.
I am her friend. I love her dearly.
I will do anything to ease her pain.
Nurse, make her come out to us.
Tell her we are on her side.

But hurry. I am afraid for . . . for those inside. This
rage will swell and burst in its own fury.

NURSE: I will do my best. But I do not expect to persuade her. Whenever any slave goes near her,
or tries to speak, her eyes burn—like those of a
lioness guarding her cubs.

(Nurse begins to exit and then says)

The men of the past were not much more than
fools, if you ask me.
They invented music, the calming sweetness of
song.
They made music at their feasts and celebrations.
But no one made music that could soothe the sor-
rows of the soul.
Sorrow eats at the heart.
It festers
And brings death.
Families fall and love ends.
If music could soothe the sorrows of the soul
It would be beyond precious.
But no.
After men have eaten well, why do they make
music?
Fat and full they're happy enough.

(exit Nurse)

CHORUS: I heard her sobbing low
Weeping deep,
Crying hard tears against the husband
Who betrayed her.
She calls on Themis, daughter of Zeus,
Who bore witness to those promises of old.
Jason swore eternal love.
Remember. She set sail in the dark of night,
Dared the dangers of the deep,

17

Left her home in the East—
And came to Greece.

(Medea enters)

MEDEA: Women of Corinth, I have come out to speak
to you because I do not want you to find fault
with me. Pride is common enough everywhere.
But sometimes people are accused of being ar-
rogant simply because they live a quiet life. The
world is quick to blame. Truth means nothing.
People have no patience. They will not wait to
find out a man's true character.
They look—and they hate.
If you're a foreigner, you should try to fit in. Even
a Greek should conform. I have accepted my
place here amongst you. But what they have
done to me I never expected, and it has broken
my heart.
My dear friends, life is nothing to me now. I want to
die. Jason was life itself to me.
And he knows that deep in his heart.
All I can feel now is utter loathing.
Of all the creatures on this living earth, we women
should be pitied most. With our rich dowries we
buy a husband. We buy—they own. They take
our bodies.
One injustice breeds another. But even then a
question lingers: Will the man be bad or good?
Divorce means eternal shame for women. To resist
the husband—unthinkable.
I was a foreigner. The laws, the customs here were
new to me. I needed magic to divine what I had
never known—how to share my husband's bed.
If we are successful, if the marriage bonds hold together a happy husband and a wife, then we are
envied.
But if not—death is better.

18

A husband can grow tired of his wife. He can leave home and find comfort somewhere else. We wives are bound to one man only. They say to us that they are the warriors—they protect us. But they are fools. I would fight three times in battle rather than give birth but once.

I am talking about me.

You have the protection of your father's house. You live a happy life, enjoy your friends. I have no city. I am alone. My husband scorns my very being.

Jason took me from my home at the edge of the earth. I have no mother, no brother, no family left to help me now.

I ask only one thing: if I can take vengeance on Jason for what he has done to me—say nothing.

Women are weak—we are not brave. When we hear the roar of battle, see the flash of steel, we cringe. But when a woman's marriage is at stake there is no creature more ready for blood.

CHORUS: I will do as you ask. It is right to punish Jason. I understand how you feel. You have been wronged.

Medea! Look, here comes Creon, king of Corinth. He must have made some new decision.

CREON: You there! Medea! Your anger against your husband is written all over your face.

I order you to leave Corinth. You and your sons must go into exile. You must leave immediately. I am here personally to see that decree is obeyed. I will not return to my palace until I am sure that you have left the city limits.

MEDEA: This is the end. I curse my life. My enemies are sailing with the wind. But there is no safe shore for me. My life is as nothing.

I have been the one who was wronged. So why do you banish me?

CREON: I am afraid of you. Why hide the truth? I am afraid that you will harm my daughter—do something that cannot be undone.
Why do I feel such fear?
Well, you are a clever woman. You know the black arts. And—you are in a fury because Jason has banned you from his bed.
I have heard that you have made threats against your husband—and against my daughter—and indeed me.
I will strike first. In self-defense.
You are free to hate me now.
But I will not be weak and later pay with tears.

MEDEA: Again it is my reputation! Again it is my curse, my destruction. If a father loves his children, he should never teach them to be too clever. Intelligence means nothing.
First of all, you never think of yourself. People are suspicious and hate you. If you talk to some fool, tell him something he doesn't understand, he will call you an incompetent and a cheat.
Talk to those with a reputation for intelligence and they will resent you—if they think that you are cleverer than they are. This has happened to me. People resent me because I am clever. But it is unfair. My skills do not run so deep.
Creon, of what are you afraid? That I might harm you? How can I—a woman—harm a king? I have no such power. Do not fear me. You have done me no wrong. You chose a husband for your daughter. You had every right to do so. True, I hate my husband. But I do not resent *your* happiness. Marry off your daughter. My blessings on you both.

But let me live here in Corinth. I will bury my
wrongs in silence.
I yield to the power of my superiors.

CREON: You speak gently. But I feel a chill in my bones
when I think of what you may be plotting deep in
your heart. In fact I'm more afraid of you now
than I was before. You know where you stand
when a woman is angry to your face—a man too.
It's the quiet devious ones you have to watch.
So, you have to leave. Now! No more discussion.
My mind's made up. You are my enemy, and you
will not trick me into letting you stay here in
Corinth.

MEDEA: I kneel before you. I beg you in the name of
your child—Jason's bride.

CREON: You are wasting your time. I will never change
my mind.

MEDEA: I beg you. Have you no pity? Will you banish
me?

CREON: I will. I love my family more than I love you.

MEDEA: Ah, my family, my home, my country! All I
think of now is you!

CREON: I love this country too—next to my daughter.

MEDEA: Love! Ha! What pain it can bring in this life.

CREON: Perhaps. That depends. Perhaps.

MEDEA: Zeus! Lord! Never forget who caused all this
pain.

CREON: Go now, and take my troubles with you.

MEDEA: Why would I need more than what I have?

CREON: In one minute I'll have you thrown out by the
scruff of your neck. Guards!

MEDEA: No, no! Wait! I ask only one thing.

CREON: More, more, always more!

MEDEA: I will go. I no longer ask to stay.

CREON: Then why are you still here? Why have you not left?

MEDEA: I ask you to give me one day. I must find a safe place to live in exile.
I must think of my two sons. I know their father will not help.
Pity me. You have a child. You should feel some sense of pity. For me exile means nothing. I weep for *them* and their suffering.

CREON: I do not have a tyrant's heart. In fact, my kindness has often gotten me into trouble. And I know that what I am about to do is perhaps unwise: I grant your request.
But I warn you, Medea, if the holy light of tomorrow's sun finds you or your sons still here, you will die. I swear this on my life. One day. That is all.
I am afraid—but one day cannot do too much harm.

(exit Creon)

CHORUS: Medea! Ah Medea! I weep for your broken heart. Where will you go? Who will take you in? The seas that you must cross rage with danger.

MEDEA: Yes, I am in danger, that is true.
But don't think that things will end up where they are now. This newly married couple will see a storm of trouble. And those who love them will not be too happy either.
Do you think I would have groveled like that before the king if I did not have a plan? No. I would have said nothing. I would not have touched

22

him. But he—oh what a fool—he has given me a day. A day! If he had banished me now, right now, he would have thwarted all my plans.

So. Now. This day will see the death of all my enemies.

Death to the king, his daughter, and my husband.

I have many ways to kill them. I do not know which to choose. Set fire to the palace? Send the bridal chamber up in flames? Or move, imperceptively, to their bedside and thrust my dagger into their guts?

There is only one thing I am afraid of: being caught as I enter the house or while setting the fire. They'd kill me on the spot and my enemies would have the last laugh. The simplest way is best. Death by poison. In that I am an expert.

So . . . let's say they are dead . . . what city will take me in? What friend do I have to offer me safety and sanctuary?

None.

But I will wait.

Such a man, a man who will protect me will come, and then I'll kill them. It will be quick, quiet, cunning.

But if Fate does not provide an escape, I will take a sword, steel my soul, and kill them both—even though I myself will surely die.

Hecate, Queen of Darkness, I worship you. You are my accomplice. My hearth is your altar. I adore you. None of them will do me harm and live to tell of it.

Help me now! This marriage will hurt them to the heart. Pain will sear their souls.

They have made a match that will curse them forever. My exile will be their eternal anguish.

But that is enough of words. Make your plans, Medea.

Your mind must seethe and scheme.
Let the moment come! Courage!
Never forget that your father was a king.
And his father was the God of the Sun.
Never forget.
Jason—the seed of Sisyphus—must not hiss his se-
cret laughter!
Courage! Let the moment come!
Besides. . . . *(to the Chorus)*
We are women, born not to live an honest life—but
to breed evil and pain.

CHORUS: The waters of our sacred streams flow back-
ward to their source.
Our laws, traditions, all things are reversed.
Men have dealt in treachery.
Men have sworn and lied.
They have dishonored the gods.
But the Voice of Time will change.
And we will live in glory forever.
The lies, the slander of our sex will fade and die.

Long ago poets sang of us.
They sang of women faithless and untrue.
Their songs will die, faithless and untrue.

Apollo, Lord of Music, you never blessed our
women's hearts
With the gift of song.
Then we could have sung the stories—
Then we could have sung the epic tales—
In scorn of men.
Time is an old god.
And Time has seen the warring blood
Between Man and Woman.
Medea, maddened by love,
You set sail through the Rocks that Thunder,
Far from your father's home.

Now, in this land of strangers,
You find your marriage broken,
Your bed deserted,
Your voice now stilled.
You are an exile.

The sanctity of oaths sworn in peace
Is violated.
Honor has deserted the wide world of the Greeks,
Has disappeared into the thin, thin air.

Where can you turn?
Who will protect you?
Your father's house is yours no more.
Another woman lies soft in your husband's bed.
A new queen reigns in your place.

(enter Jason)

JASON: I have seen this before—this is not the first
time.
Uncontrolled anger—such as yours—is deadly.
You could have stayed here in Corinth. You could
have still lived here in this house.
You should have quietly accepted the decisions of
those in power.
But no, you had to talk like a fool.
So, you are banished. Listen, nothing you say in
your anger can upset *me*.
You can charge me with crime after crime, for as
long as you like.
But you attacked the king and the princess!
You are lucky to get off with exile!
I tried my best to calm them down. But you, fool
that you are, keep up your assaults on the royal
family.
So, you are banished.
However, I still care for you and I will not desert
you.

I have given a great deal of thought about your future. And despite everything I am here to make sure that you and the children are not sent away unprovided for.

You will need money. Exile will be hard.

I know you must hate me. But I could never feel anything but care for you.

MEDEA: You disgusting coward! What else am I to call a man who is no man? So, you have come to face me, my worst enemy. That's not courage—that's an insult. You may think yourself brave facing the family you have betrayed. But no, you are sick, sick to the soul. For you have no conscience. But there is one good thing about your coming here. Now I can ease the pain in my heart by confronting you with your wickedness. And when you hear me speak it will make you wince.

Let me begin at the beginning. I saved your life. Every Greek who sailed with you on the *Argo* knows this to be a fact. You were sent to tame the bulls that breathe fire, put them under the yoke, and sow the earth with the seeds of death. But it was I who killed the serpent who guarded the Golden Fleece. I killed that living mass of seething coils which never slept, killed it and saved your life. Then, for you, for love of you, mad fool that I was, I betrayed my own father and the brothers whom I loved and came with you to Iolchos. And for you I brought the most unimaginable death upon King Pelias, death at the hands of his own daughters. Oh when I was by your side you had nothing to fear. And how did you repay all that I had done for you? You took a new wife. Foul lump of a man, you betrayed the mother of your children. If we had been childless, I could have forgiven you for marrying again. But I bore you children. Where is the respect for the undying oaths which you swore? I do not understand you. Do you no longer believe in our ancient gods? Have right and wrong lost their meaning? You must know in your heart that you have broken every promise you made to me. Look at this hand! You touched it and promised to be true! You clung to my knees and swore eternal love. But you, false husband that you are, defiled everything you touched and left me in despair.

But let's pretend that we are friends, let me ask you for advice—not that I expect any help from you. But let that pass. I will ask you and expose you for the coward that you are. Where am I to go? Home to my father? I betrayed my home and my country when I left them to come here with you. Maybe I should go to the wretched daughters of Pelias. They'd give me a royal welcome sure enough. I murdered their father. This is the reality: the ones that I love at home now hate me; and because I helped you, those whom I had no right to hurt hate me too.

And what is my reward? You have made me the envy of every Greek woman alive! What a marvelous, faithful husband I have! I am only being sent into exile, thrown out of the country without a friend beside me, all alone with my abandoned children. Oh you will be a living scandal when the world sees you happily married while your own sons and the woman who saved your life wander begging by the roadside. Oh Zeus! You gave us the power to tell true gold from counterfeit. Why is there no mark upon human flesh to tell that the heart within is false and rotten?

CHORUS LEADER: When those who loved each other
once
Begin to quarrel
Terrible is the anger
And hard to heal.

JASON: It looks as though I will need a great deal of skill to ride this out. I will have to be a clever helmsman and haul in my sails if I am going to escape the storm of your abuse.
To begin with, you are making a mountain of exaggeration about what you did for me. I believe with all my heart that it was Aphrodite, goddess of love, and Aphrodite alone who protected me on my journey. You are a very clever woman, but it would be ungentlemanly of me to argue that it was passion that drove you to save my life. So I will not dwell on that particular fact. If you managed to help me here and there, that's all well and good. But as I shall prove, by protecting me you got far more than you gave. Let me just point out, first of all, that you are now living in Greece, not in a land of barbarians. Here you have known Justice, not brute force. Throughout Greece you are recognized as a woman with extraordinary skills. You are famous. If you were still living at the ends of the earth, no one would ever have heard of you. Fame! I'd never choose gold or musical skill surpassing Orpheus if the world knew nothing of my life. *You* brought up the issue of my journey to fetch the Golden Fleece, and that is my answer. Now, to turn to the question of my marriage to the princess—which you have thrown in my face. I shall prove first that it was a clever move, second that it was the

sensible thing to do, and third that I did it in the interest of you and the children. Do not interrupt me. When I came here from Iolchos I brought with me a mountain of difficulties. What better solution could I have found than marriage to the king's daughter? I was an exile, a foreigner. It was not that I had grown tired of you—I know that it's *that* which eats away at you—no, I hadn't fallen desperately in love with a younger woman. And I certainly was not interested in having more children. The sons that we have are enough. I have no criticism of you in that area. All that I wanted was to give us security and prosperity. A poor man has no influence, no friends. Furthermore I wanted to bring up my children in a manner befitting my station in life and to give them new brothers and unite both our families in prosperity. You don't need any more children, and I would be glad to help ours by fathering more. That wasn't such a bad plan was it? You would be the first to agree if you weren't eaten away by jealousy. You're like all women—if your marriage is good then life is good. But if your husband doesn't share your bed anymore, what was good turns to bitterness and gall. If only children could come into this world some other way—without the female sex! This world would be a much happier place.

CHORUS LEADER: Jason, you are a clever speaker. But, like it or not, I have to say that you have done wrong in abandoning your wife.

MEDEA: I do not share most people's opinions . . . and my view is that a wicked man who can make an eloquent defense of his actions is the most loathsome creature of all. He is so confident that he can get away with anything—he believes that his oily

29

tongue will make sure that he slithers out of any crime. But there is a limit to his cleverness—and yes, all this applies to you. Don't think for a moment that you have made your case—for all your fine words. One word will undo you. If you had any sense of honor you would have sought my *consent*. You wouldn't have married behind my back.

JASON: Oh I'm sure if I had brought it up you would have been *most* helpful. Look at you. You still can't control your foul temper.

MEDEA: That's not why. You had a foreign wife who was no longer young, and you were looking for *respect*.

JASON: Listen to me once and for all—I made this match without any desire for the girl. As I told you before, I wanted to protect you, father princes to be brothers to my sons, and secure the prosperity of our family.

MEDEA: If that's prosperity, I want none of it. If that's happiness, keep it away from my heart.

JASON: You can change that wish and the world will think you wise. Prosperity is a blessing, happiness no curse.

MEDEA: Don't mock me. You have a bed to sleep in. I must wander the homeless earth.

JASON: That was your own choice. Don't blame anyone else.

MEDEA: My choice? What did I do? Leave you and marry somebody else?

JASON: You made the wicked mistake of cursing the king.

MEDEA: Maybe I am a curse upon your house.

JASON: End of argument. I have nothing more to say to you. If you need anything from me to help you and the children, I will give it and be generous. I will also write to friends of mine abroad, and I'm sure they will help you. If you reject this offer, my dear woman, you will really be a fool. It will be much better for you if you can forget your anger.

MEDEA: I would never accept help from your friends. And I would never take a thing from you. Don't even offer it. You're a liar and a traitor. Your charity means nothing.

JASON: Well, I call on the gods to witness that I have offered every assistance to you and the children. I have been kind, and you have not responded. In fact, you have rejected all offers of friendship. You will only suffer more than you have to.

(exit Jason)

MEDEA: Yes. Go! Don't wait around here. You are burning with desire for your latest catch. Go! Enjoy her!
But, god be my witness, one day soon you will regret this marriage.

CHORUS: Love that comes violent,
   That comes in excess,
   Comes with no honor
   Comes with no grace.

   But if she comes gentle
   Bathed in her light
   There is nothing more joyful
   More steeped in delight.

   But never, oh never,
   Aphrodite my queen
   Aim your bow at my heart

With your arrows so keen.
Passion is a golden dart
That no man can escape.

Let a moderate life be mine
For that I will thank the gods.

May Aphrodite never pierce my heart
With longing for another man.
Peace and loving silence is what I crave
Upon our marriage.
Respect the bed
Where love means silent peace.

Oh my home, my country,
I pray your arms will hold me
Forever.
To be an exile is to be
Without hope,
Without pity.

Better death. Yes, death before exile.
No pain is worse
Than to be without a home.

Medea! This I have seen,
Seen the awful pity,
Seen your anguish
As you leave the city.
Forever alone.

I give you my heart
(For love is not blind)
As you are forced to part
From friends who love you.
And will love you
Forever
Alone.

(enter Aegeus)

AEGEUS: Happiness be with you, Medea. What better wish for a friend?

MEDEA: And happiness to you, Aegeus, son of Pandion the Wise. Where have you come from?

AEGEUS: I have just left the ancient oracle of Apollo.

MEDEA: The center of the earth. What help were you seeking there, in the home of prophecy?

AEGEUS: I asked the god how I might father a child.

MEDEA: Have you lived all these years without conceiving a child?

AEGEUS: Yes. That seems to be the will of some god.

MEDEA: Are you married or are you still . . . ?

AEGEUS: I have a wife to share my bed.

MEDEA: What did Apollo say to you about having children?

AEGEUS: His answer was too subtle for me or any man to understand.

MEDEA: Is it permissible for me to hear it?

AEGEUS: It is. Believe me, it needs an intelligence such as yours to interpret it.

MEDEA: Then tell me—since it is permitted.

AEGEUS: He ordered me "not to unstop the neck of the wineskin"—

MEDEA: Until. . . .

AEGEUS: Until I return to the home where I was born.

MEDEA: Then why are you traveling through Corinth?

AEGEUS: First I need to visit Pittheus, king of Troezen . . .

MEDEA: The son of Pelops, yes, a very holy man.

AEGEUS: I want to ask his advice about the oracle.

MEDEA: He is a wise man and is well versed in such things.

AEGEUS: And of all my friends I love him the most. We fought in the wars together.

MEDEA: I wish you luck. May you get all your heart desires.

AEGEUS: But tell me. Your eyes are sad, your face so pale . . . why?

MEDEA: Aegeus, I have the most cruel husband in the world.

AEGEUS: I don't understand. Tell me what your trouble is.

MEDEA: Jason has wronged me—the wife who has always been by his side.

AEGEUS: What has he done? Tell me.

MEDEA: He has taken another wife. She is now the mistress of *my* house.

AEGEUS: That is disgraceful. Do you mean that he actually . . . ?

MEDEA: Yes, I do. He loved me once. Now he has left me.

AEGEUS: Did he grow tired of you? Or did he fall in love with someone else?

MEDEA: Someone else . . . passionately. He betrays those who love him.

AEGEUS: Well, if he's as bad as you say, let him go.

MEDEA: He's fallen in love with the power of a king.

AEGEUS: Who is the girl's father?

MEDEA: Creon, king of Corinth.

AEGEUS: I see. Now I understand why you are so angry.

MEDEA: It is the end of everything. But there is more. I am being sent into exile.

AEGEUS: By whom? This is beyond bearing.

MEDEA: By Creon. I must leave his kingdom.

AEGEUS: And Jason agrees to this? Disgraceful!

MEDEA: Oh he pretends that he doesn't. But he'll pull through. I am your suppliant. See! I touch your beard and throw myself at your feet. Pity me, pity me in my misery. I am an exile. I cannot survive without friends. Let me find refuge with you in Athens. Let me be welcome in your house. If you do, the gods may give you the children you desire and you would die a happy man. It is good fortune that brought you here. You will be childless no longer. I will make you the father of generations to come. I have the power. I know the magic potions that can do it.

AEGEUS: I have many reasons to do this favor for you, Medea. First, out of respect for the gods. Then there is your promise of children—for I have done all that I can with no success. This is what I am prepared to do: if you can get to Athens by yourself, I promise I will do all in my power to protect you. But I must be blunt. I cannot take you with me out of Corinth. If you reach my palace, you will find sanctuary there. I will never hand you over to anybody. But I am a friend of the Corinthians. I cannot risk offending my hosts.

MEDEA: I understand. Now if you will swear on oath what you have promised, I will be satisfied.

35

AEGEUS: Don't you trust me? What more do you need?

MEDEA: I trust you. But I have many enemies . . . not only Creon but the daughters of Pelias also. If you swore on oath, I know you would never surrender me to them if they demanded my return. But words alone are not enough. I need a sacred pledge. Otherwise you might be persuaded to become their ally. I have no influence. I have no power. They have the wealth and authority of a royal house.

AEGEUS: I respect your taking these precautions. And I will not refuse you. It will, in fact, be safer for me this way. I will have an excuse to offer to your enemies. And you will be all the more secure. What are the terms of the oath?

MEDEA: That you will never cast me out of Athens and never, willingly, while you are alive, surrender me to any of my enemies who want to seize me.

AEGEUS: I swear by the Earth and the Holy Light of the Sun . . . by all the gods to keep the terms of this oath.

MEDEA: I am satisfied. But if you break this oath, what then?

AEGEUS: May the gods punish me with the violence I would deserve.

MEDEA: Go on your way, and good luck be with you. All is well. I will come to Athens as quickly as I can—when I have done what I must do and filled the desires of my heart.

(Aegeus exits)

CHORUS LEADER: May Hermes, protector of travelers, bring you home in safety. And may you too fill the desires of your heart. We bless a man of such nobility.

MEDEA: O Zeus, Protector of Justice! O Light of the Sun! The time is coming, my friends, when I will sing a song of victory over my enemies. I am moving on the path that will lay them low. They will be punished. Now there is hope. Just when I needed him most, this man came to me, a harbor from the storm. There in Athens I will cast the anchor of my safety.

Now I will tell you all my plans. What you are about to hear is deadly earnest. I will send one of my servants to ask Jason to come to see me. When he comes, I will be submissive, my tongue will be gentle. I will tell him that I have come to understand what he has done and that I approve of his concern for us. I will ask him only this: that he allow our children to remain behind. Not that I would leave my sons on enemy soil for them to insult. No! I need them for my plan to kill the princess. I will send them to her with bridal gifts, an exquisite robe and a crown of beaten gold, an offering to save them from exile. When she puts on this glorious finery, she will die in agony—she and anyone who touches her. For I will steep these gifts in deadly poison.

But enough of that. What I must do then tears at my heart. I must kill my children, the children that I love. No one will ever take them away from me. Then, oh then, the house of Jason will be utterly destroyed. And I will escape from Corinth, leaving behind me my own, my sweet sweet children, murdered. Guilt I can face, the laughter of my enemies never.

So be it. What do I have to live for? I have no father, no home, no place to hide. I was a fool all those years ago when I left my father's palace. But I was won over by the smooth words of a Greek. But now with god's help he will be punished. He will never again set eyes upon those sons that I bore him. Never will he father sons by his new bride. She will die by my poisons, die an agonizing death. No one will look down on me and scorn me for being weak or passive. No! I am a different breed, loyal to my friends and dangerous to my enemies. My life is beyond glory.

CHORUS LEADER: You confided in me, and I would like to be of help to you. But there are laws that govern human beings. I beg you do not do this.

MEDEA: There is no other way. But I sympathize with you. Just remember that I, not you, have been terribly wronged.

CHORUS LEADER: But—to kill your own children! How can you have the heart to do it?

MEDEA: This is the only way to torture and get revenge upon my husband.

CHORUS LEADER: But it is the way that will make you the unhappiest woman in the world.

MEDEA: Enough. Until it is done words are meaningless. *(perhaps to the Nurse)* Go and bring Jason here. I have always trusted you. Say nothing of what you have heard. You too are a woman and a loyal servant to your mistress.

CHORUS: The sons of Athens have been blessed
Time out of mind.
Children of the gods,
They found life in a holy land,
A land untouched by war.
They feed on Wisdom's fruits.

There, beneath the ever shining skies,
They walk in grace.
There, where once Golden Harmony
Gave birth to the Muses of Pieria.
So goes the story.

Aphrodite dips her cup
In the clear streams of Cephisus
And waters the gentle land.
She breathes her soft and fragrant
Breath over the sweet earth.
Her flowing hair is crowned with
Perfumed roses,
And she sends her Loves to sit beside
The Wisdom of the ages,
Creating Beauty everywhere.
So goes the story.

How then will this holy land,
This welcoming land,
Watered by pure streams,
Take you into its arms
When you have killed
Your own flesh?
You will pollute that sacred soil!
Think of the knife at the throat,
Think of the blood soaking the earth!
On our knees we beg you,
By all the gods we beg you,
Do not kill your children.

How will you harden your heart?
How, when you look in their eyes,
Will you drive in the knife
At the moment of death?
When they look up at you,
Will you not weep
At the moment of death?

When your sons kneel down before you,
When they beg for their life,
Will you dip your fingers in their blood?
No, your heart will melt,
And you will relent.

(enter Jason and Nurse)

JASON: You sent for me and I have come. I know you hate me, but I will listen to what you have to say. What is it you want of me?

MEDEA: Jason, forgive me for all the things I said. You and I have shared many happy times together. So I ask you to overlook my violent outburst. I have been thinking things over. In fact, I took myself to task. "You fool!" I said to myself. "Do you have no sense? Why do you attack those who are trying to help you? Why pick a quarrel with the king and with your husband? What he is doing can only help us if he marries a princess and gets royal brothers for our children. What is the matter with you? Why are you still angry? After all, the gods are providing for you. You have the children to think of. You are already an exile from your own country. You need all the friends you can get."

When I thought the matter through this way, I came to realize how blind I'd been and how foolish my resentment. And so I wanted to thank you. I think you were very wise to form this alliance. I was the fool. I ought to have helped you with your plans. In fact I should have prepared the very marriage bed and been of service to the new bride. But I am what I am, a woman. I will leave it at that. So, Jason, be a man, and don't sink to a woman's pettiness. You needn't copy my mistakes. I beg your pardon. I admit that I was wrong. But now, as you see, I have changed for the better.

Children! Children! Come outside to see your father! *(the children enter with the Tutor)* There! Kiss your father. Talk to him as I am doing, and tell him we are friends again. We're not angry anymore. There now! Hold him by the hand.

Oh but I am afraid of what the future holds. My children, will you stretch your arms out like that for all eternity? My heart is racked with grief. I cannot hold back the tears. I have made my peace with your father, and now I have wet this sweet face with my tears.

CHORUS: I too cannot help weeping. Oh let there be no more cause for grief.

JASON: I am pleased, Medea, that you have changed your mind.

I can and do forgive your past resentment. It is natural when a husband takes a second wife. But you have reasoned your case well and realized how vulnerable you were. It took some time, but it was a wise decision. My sons, your father has been planning for your future, and with the help of the gods you will have a good life. In time I know that you and your new brothers will be leading men here in Corinth. Just grow big and strong. Your father and those gods who are his friends will do the rest. When you are strong grown men, may I see you triumph over my enemies.

(to Medea who is weeping)

What's this? Why this flood of tears? Why do you look so pale? Aren't you happy when I talk like this?

41

MEDEA: It is nothing. I was thinking of my children.

JASON: Do not weep for them. I will take care of them.

MEDEA: I do not doubt your word. But women are women—it is our nature to weep.

JASON: But why do you grieve over the children?

MEDEA: I am their mother. When you were praying for their future, I was thinking of what might happen to them, and I felt a pain in my heart.
But I have not told you all I had to say. Creon is sending me into exile. That is the right thing to do. I know that if I remained I might be a source of conflict between you and him. People think of me as an enemy to you all. So I should leave.
But I want the children to be brought up in your care. Beg Creon to let them stay.

JASON: I don't know if he will listen to me. But I will do my best.

MEDEA: Why don't you ask your wife to speak on their behalf?

JASON: I will. I'm sure I can persuade her.

MEDEA: You will if she is like other women. But I will help you. I will send the children with gifts for her, the most beautiful gifts imaginable. Bring me the robe and crown of gold. Be quick. She will be bathed in happiness. Not only will she have you for a husband, but she will wear these treasures which the Sun, my father's father, gave to his descendants. *(Medea takes a casket and hands it to the children)*
Children, take these wedding gifts to the happy bride. Give them to her. They are everything that she deserves.

JASON: That's very foolish of you. Why deprive your-self of such treasures? Especially now. The royal palace is rich in gold and robes. Keep them for yourself. Don't give them away. If my wife has any respect for me at all, she will listen to me. There is no need for such rich gifts.

MEDEA: Let me do it. They say that gifts can persuade even the gods. Gold can speak louder than ten thousand words. The day belongs to her. And soon her fortune will grow even more. She is young. She is a princess. I would give my life to save my sons from exile. Gold is nothing.
Come my children. You must go into the palace. Kneel down before your father's new wife, the daughter of the king, and beg her to save you from exile. Give her this gift. Put it into her hands. That is very important. Go as fast as you can. May your mission be successful. Come back to me with the news I long to hear.

(exeunt Jason, the Tutor, and the children)

CHORUS: Now my hopes lie dead.
The children cannot live.
Already they walk the road of death.
She will take the golden crown,
Take the circle of doom.
She will place it on her head—
Ah poor creature—
And death will smile
In the gold of her hair.

The sheer beauty of the dress,
The glistening of the crown
Will seduce her young eyes.
She will wear them as a bride.
She will be the bride of Death.
Into this net of doom she will fall.

43

Trapped in the snares of blood
She cannot escape.

I pity you, Jason, pity
Your marriage of pain.

You see nothing, nothing
Of sons slaughtered,
Of a bride torn by bloody fire.
You wretched man,
So sure of your happiness
So steeped in sorrow.

I pity you, Medea, pity
Your mother's heart.
For a bed betrayed
You will kill your sons.
Your husband sleeps
in a royal bed.
And you will kill your sons.

(the Tutor returns with the children)

TUTOR: Mistress, here are your children. They are no longer condemned to exile. The princess took the gifts in her own hands and was delighted. So the children are safe. What's the matter? Why do you stand there all sad and dejected? This is good news!

MEDEA: Ah the pain that I feel!

TUTOR: That's not the way to respond to the news I brought.

MEDEA: The pain is too much to bear.

TUTOR: Did I tell you something awful—without realizing it? I thought it was good. Was I wrong?

MEDEA: What you had to say was . . . what you had to say. I am not blaming you.

44

TUTOR: Then why are you just staring at the ground, your eyes streaming with tears?

MEDEA: My dear old friend, I have no choice but tears. The gods have done this. And I have done a terrible thing.

TUTOR: Take heart, take heart. Some day your children will bring you home again.

MEDEA: Before that day I will find a different home for *all* of them.

TUTOR: You are not the first woman to be parted from her children. We are all mortal, and we must live with pain.

MEDEA: Yes, there is truth in what you say.
Now go inside and get things ready for the boys—as you do every . . . other day.

(exit Tutor)

MEDEA: Oh my children, my children. You now have a city to live in. You have a home for as long as you live. But you will have no mother beside you. I must leave you in all my grief. I must be an exile in a strange land. I will never taste the joy of your happiness. I will never watch you growing up, never see you on your wedding day, never decorate your marriage beds or hold the wedding torches high in the air.
I have a will of iron that has brought this misery upon me.
But I will not relent.
I remember the pains that racked my body in the agony of your birth. I remember the aching joy of caring for you. Was it all for nothing? Once, oh once, I had great hopes for you. I dreamed that you would comfort me when I was old and,

45

when I died, would wrap me tenderly and make me ready for my grave. The world would envy me for my two sons. But that sweet sad dream has faded now. I must leave you and lead my own bitter and lonely life. You will never look upon your mother's face again with those eyes that I love so much. You will be so far far away from me.

Oh god, don't look at me like that, my children. Why are you smiling? Why? Your last smile. . . .

(to the Chorus)

What am I to do? All my courage is gone. When I see their bright, young faces—I can't do it. All my plans were for nothing. I'll take them with me away from here. Why should I hurt them? To make their father suffer, why should I suffer twice as much as he?

No, I will not do it. I care nothing for my plans.

But what am I thinking? Are my enemies going to have the last laugh? Are they to go unpunished? No, I must find the courage. I am a coward if I let such weak thoughts enter my brain. Boys, go inside. *(the children move at least out of earshot, perhaps actually into the palace; to the Chorus—using the formal language of the ritual of animal sacrifice)* If there be anyone here whose presence will profane my sacrifice, let them beware. My hand will not falter.

Oh my heart, do not do it! You cruel fool, let them live, let them live. Yes, we'll all live safe together in the city of Athens. We will be happy together. . . .

No, by all the avenging spirits of Hell, no! no! no! My sons will never live to be the victims of the fury of my enemies. There is no way out. They must die.

46

In any case, the thing is done. Even now the crown
   is on her head and the robe is eating at her flesh
   and she is dying. I can see it, I can see it! I have
   begun my sad journey, and it is time for them to
   go on theirs. I must speak to them once more.

(the children draw close)

Give your mother your hands, my children. Let me
   kiss them. Oh sweet hands, sweet lips. Let me
   look at you, let me look at those innocent brave
   faces. May you find happiness—but there, not
   here. Your father has killed all the happiness we
   could have had here. Oh how I love to touch
   you. Oh your skin is so soft to touch, your breath
   so sweet. Oh my babies!
Go now, go. I cannot bear to look at you anymore.

(the children exit)

My grief overwhelms me. I understand the horror
   of what I must do. But passion is stronger than
   reason, and passion is the grief of the world.

CHORUS: Though I am a woman,
   Often have I thought deep thoughts
   About this life,
   Often struggled with its mysteries.
   For we too are blessed with a mind
   That seeks a human truth.
   Not all of us, perhaps, but a happy few
   Are proud lovers of wisdom's grace.

And my mind now tells me this—
   Those who are childless
   Are the happiest of mortals.
   To be childless is to be free,
   Free from the knowledge
   Of whether your children

Are a blessing or a curse
Free from a life of pain.

I see those whose young grow strong
In a home filled with love.
Day by day
I see them burdened with care.
For they must mold an honest human soul
While struggling to provide a means to live.
Then this—will all their labor
Be for a good or worthless child?

But the crowning grief is this:
The child is grown and strong,
Honest and provided for,
Then if the whim of Fate
So chooses, Death comes.
Death takes the child into darkness.
Why then breed a life of love
If the gods breed death
And crown this life
With the greatest grief of all?
The death of a child.
The death of a child.

MEDEA: All this time I have been waiting, waiting to see what will happen, watching, watching the palace doors. Ah! Now! One of Jason's servants! Out of breath and with news of horror and of death.

(enter Messenger)

MESSENGER: Medea, you have committed a crime unholy and unspeakable. Get away, chariot or ship, it doesn't matter, but get away.

MEDEA: No, tell me first why I should run.

MESSENGER: The princess is dead. Her father too, murdered by your poisons.

MEDEA: There could be no better news. Now and forever I count you my friend and savior.

MESSENGER: What? What are you saying? Are you out of your mind? You have committed this crime, beyond all horror, against the royal house. And yet you rejoice and are not afraid?

MEDEA: I could answer that. But take your time, my friend. Tell me everything. How did they die? My pleasure will be twice as much if they died in agony.

MESSENGER: When your children came to the palace with their father and entered the quarters where the princess lived, we were all happy—those of us who had been saddened by your troubles. A whisper ran around the room, from ear to ear, that you had patched up your quarrel with Jason. One of us kissed your children's hands, another their hair. I was so happy. I personally took them into the women's rooms. The mistress—yes we now call her that in your place—didn't see the boys at first. She had eyes only for Jason. Then— I suppose she resented the children's presence—she covered her eyes with a veil and turned her face away.
Your husband tried to make peace with her. "Don't be angry with those who love you," he said. "Calm down and turn to look at us. You must think of those who love me as your friends too. They bring you gifts. Take them and for me, for me, ask your father not to send them into exile." When she saw the beauty of the gifts, she could not resist. She promised her husband all that he asked, and almost before he and the children had left she took the robe in all its finery and put it on. Then she took the crown and put it on her falling curls—in fact she began to arrange her

hair in a mirror, smiling at the dead image in the glass. She got up and began to stroll through the rooms, her feet white and bare, moving with a kind of delicacy and overjoyed with the gifts. Time and again she would stand on tiptoe and look down on the folds that caressed her ankles. Then it happened. What we saw was terror. She suddenly turned deathly white. She staggered, turned, her whole body in convulsions, and collapsed into a chair or she would have fallen to the ground. One old servant, thinking it was a seizure of some kind, something god-sent anyway, I suppose, began to pray. Then she saw the white foam bubbling from her mouth, her eyes rolling in their sockets, and the blood draining from her cheeks, and she began to scream. No more prayers, just a scream of grief. The mourning had begun.

One servant ran to Creon's palace, another to find Jason to tell him of what was happening to his wife. The whole house echoed with the sound of footsteps running, running. All this happened so quickly—as quick as a fast runner could circle the track. The girl was lying there, her eyes closed and not making a sound. Suddenly she screamed and came to. She was attacked on two fronts. The golden crown on her head burned with an eerie flow of fire. The robe, which your children had brought, began to eat at her soft flesh. She was now all in flames. She got up and ran. She was tearing at her hair, trying to dislodge the crown. But the circle of gold seemed to tighten its grip, and as she tossed her hair the flames blazed all the more fiercely. In agony she fell to the ground. Only a father could have recognized her now. Her eyes, her face were a mass of fused flesh. Her blood was on fire and dripped in thick clots from her skull. Her flesh oozed from her bones—like resin from a pine tree—eaten raw by the fangs of the poison. It was a terrible sight. Everyone was afraid to touch her, for they had learned too well from what they saw.

Then her father—oh the poor man—suddenly came into the room. He didn't understand what was there before his eyes, and he threw himself on the body. He was sobbing as he kissed her, and he cried out, "Oh my darling, what god has done this to you? Why, oh why take my only child? I am old and ready for my grave. The cruelty of it all! Oh let me join you in death my daughter!" He stopped sobbing and silently tried to get to his feet. But, as ivy sticks fast to a laurel tree, the poor old man stuck to the robe. Oh god it was horrible to see him struggle. He tried to remove his leg, but the girl's body pulled him down. The more violently he tried to escape, the more the withered flesh was torn from his bones. After a while he ceased his struggle, gave in to his fate, and breathed his last breath. Now they are joined in death, father and daughter. It is a sight made for tears. Medea, what am I to say to you? You know yourself what you have to do to escape punishment. I have believed for a long time that human life is but a shadow. No man is truly happy. One man may be more prosperous than another if luck comes his way. But happiness does not exist.

(exit Messenger)

CHORUS LEADER: It seems that the will of the gods is at work, bringing grief upon grief to Jason. His punishment is just. But we pity the poor princess. Her marriage to Jason was a marriage with Death.

MEDEA: My friends, the time has come and I must do it quickly. I must kill my children and escape. If I delay, someone else will kill them, someone who loves them far less than I. They must die. And since they must, I who gave them life will take that life from them. Be strong, my heart. Oh why can I not move? It is a terrible thing to do, but it must be done. This hand is cursed! But take the sword! Take it! Face the moment of a misery that will never end. Be brave now. Do not let the children enter your mind. Forget that you love them, forget that you are their mother, forget, for this one short day, your own children. You have all the days to come to mourn for them. And you *will* mourn, for though you kill them, you loved them with all your heart. My life is a life of pain.

CHORUS: Oh Earth! Oh bright light of the Sun!
Look down! Look down upon this woman.
She is cursed. Stop her before she kills.
Let her not spill her children's blood.
They are sons sprung from your golden race,
Oh Light of the Sun. Blood that once flowed
In the veins of the gods should not be spilled
By mortal hands. Stop her before she kills.
Sun God, hold back her murderous hand.
Deliver the house from this avenging Fury.
Have pity on the children.

You loved them and all for nothing.
You gave them life and all for nothing.
Why did you leave your home and sail
Between the savage Rocks that Thunder?
Why does this rage poison your heart?
Why do you hunger for the blood

52

Of your blood? You loved them.
And to kill one's own child
Brings heaven's black curse.
The murder lives on forever,
Forever curses the house.
There is no escape from the pain.
That is the will of the gods.

(the children are heard within)

Listen, listen. The children are calling for help. Oh
you cruel, unhappy woman!

(ONE OF THE CHILDREN INSIDE THE PALACE): No!
Mother, no! Help us! Help us! She is going to kill
us! Where can we hide?

(THE OTHER CHILD): I love you, my brother. There is
no escape.

CHORUS: We must go in. We have to save them.

(ONE OF THE CHILDREN): Help us! For god's sake! The
knife is at my throat.

CHORUS: Woman! Your heart is made of stone.
Steel in your soul, steel in your hand,
You kill the flesh of your flesh,
The blood of your blood.

One other woman, in all of human time,
Slaughtered her own sons.
Men keep tales in their hearts
Of Ino made mad by the gods,
Hera was jealous of Zeus's lust
And made her wander the lonely earth.
Poised on a cliff's sharp edge,
She clutched her babies to her breast,
Then leapt into the unforgiving sea.
Mother and children locked in death.

53

This passes all grief.
It ices the soul.

The marriage bed is passion and pain.
On it lie all the agonies of human life.

(enter Jason)

JASON: You women! You there, by the door! Is Medea still inside? She has killed them! Is she gone? I swear that she must hide in the bowels of the earth or soar on wings into the sky if she is to escape my vengeance for what she has done to the royal house. She has killed the king and the princess. Does she think that she will not be punished? But I am thinking of my children, not her. The victims of her savagery will see to her. No, I've come to save my sons. Creon's family will kill them to avenge their mother's unspeakable crime.

CHORUS: Jason, I pity you. Your troubles are just beginning. From what you said I know you know nothing.

JASON: Troubles? Is she trying to kill me too?

CHORUS: Your sons are dead. Medea has killed them both.

JASON: Killed them? You kill me when you say that!

CHORUS: Both of them are dead.

JASON: Where? Where are they? Are they in there?

CHORUS: If you open the palace doors, you will see them lying in a pool of blood.

JASON: Open the palace doors! Open them and let me see two things—the bodies of my sons and the woman that I will kill.

(Medea is seen in a chariot, in the air, perhaps with dragons for wings. She is on the machine, *the crane that or-*

dinarily lofted a god *to provide a solution to the tragic impasse—the deus ex machina. But in this theatrical coup* she *is seen flying through the air with the bodies of her children draped over the side of the chariot.)*

MEDEA: Jason! Why are you battering at the doors? Are you looking for your children? They are dead, and I killed them. There is nothing left to do. If you have anything to *say* to me, then say it. But you cannot touch us. We are safe in this chariot which the God of the Sun has sent down to earth to save us from our enemies.

JASON: I hate you beyond all hate. You are loathed by every god, by me, by the whole human race. How could you—for god's sake you gave them life—how could you put the knife in their hearts? They were your babies! And you leave me behind without a child. My life is ruined! You have committed a crime that defies reason. Can you face Mother Earth, can you face the Sun? You pollute the earth and the heavens. May the gods blast you into oblivion!

At long last I have recovered my senses. I had lost them before. I was mad when I brought you from your palace in a land where savages rule. I brought you to Greece. I gave you a home. I gave a home to you—a living curse—you had already betrayed your father and your home. You deserved to die. But the gods have turned that death on me. When you came on board the *Argo*, you had already killed your brother, killed him there in his own home. And then you came on board my ship. You stepped onto the *Argo*, the ship that I loved. That was the beginning. You became my wife and you gave me children. But now you have taken their lives away. You were jealous of the princess, and jealousy killed them.

No Greek woman would have done this. But I chose you! I chose horror and murder for a wife, not a woman but a she-dog, a tigress, an eater of men. But why do I bother to speak? A thousand curses would not move you. You feel nothing in that heart of stone. Get out of my sight, you creature that knows no shame, you killer of your own children. Let me mourn for my lost life. I have lost my young wife, lost the children I fathered and brought up. I will never see them again.

MEDEA: If there was any use in doing so, I would have answered you point by point. But why? Zeus the Father knows everything I did for you and how you repaid me. You thought that you could defile my bed, make a fool of me and live a happy life. You were mistaken. So was the princess. So was Creon. He thought he could make you his son-in-law and then send me into exile. But he was punished too. So now I am a tigress, an eater of men? Call me what you like. I have broken your heart.

JASON: You are suffering too. Your loss is as great as mine.

MEDEA: That is true. But I am willing to pay the price just to see the smile wiped off your face.

JASON: My sons, you were cursed with a wicked mother.

MEDEA: My sons, the sins of your father cost you your lives.

JASON: This hand did not kill my children.

MEDEA: Not your hand but your treachery and lust.

JASON: You killed them because I left you? Left your bed?

MEDEA: You think that is a small thing, a thing a woman could just ignore?

JASON: Yes. If you had any sense of decency. But you are a woman who has no shame.

MEDEA: Decency! Shame! — Words! Your sons are dead!

JASON: They will live to haunt you for the rest of your life.

MEDEA: Who was the cause of all this pain? The gods know.

JASON: Yes, they know the depths to which you have sunk.

MEDEA: You can curse me, you can scream at me. All I have is loathing.

JASON: That is all I have too. Let us make an agreement and part.

MEDEA: What agreement? I will do what you want.

JASON: Give me my sons. I will bury their bodies, give them all the necessary rituals.

MEDEA: Never! I will take them to the temple of Hera of the Mountains. With my own hands I will bury them in the holy shrine itself—so that none of my enemies will ever open their grave and desecrate their bodies. And I will establish an annual festival to be celebrated by the people of Corinth. For all time to come, this will be a day of atonement for this crime against heaven. I will go to Athens, city of Erechtheus, where King Aegeus will give me refuge. And now I tell you this: you, as you deserve, will die an ignominious death, a fitting punishment for your treachery.

JASON: May the curse of your children's blood lie heavy upon you! And the Furies pursue you to your death!

MEDEA: Do you think there is a god who will listen to your prayers? You! Who lie and deceive and break your oaths!

JASON: I hate you for the brutal killer you are.

MEDEA: Go back to the palace. Your wife is waiting to be buried.

JASON: I am going, a father robbed of his children.

MEDEA: You are just beginning to grieve. You have the rest of your life to feel the pain.

JASON: Oh my children, you were loved so much!

MEDEA: By me, not by you.

JASON: If you loved them, why did you kill them?

MEDEA: To break your heart.

JASON: I long to hold them in my arms, to kiss them on the lips and ease my pain.

MEDEA: Yes. Now you speak words of love and long to kiss them. Not so long ago you were sending them into exile.

JASON: Oh let me touch their soft cheeks for the last time.

MEDEA: Never again. You waste your breath.

(the chariot begins its ascent)

JASON: Zeus! Do you hear how I am mocked?
I am left here alone.
This brute of a woman escapes,
Steeped in the blood of her children.

It is time for me to grieve.
The strength that I have left
I will pour into my tears.
You gods above, never forget
That you (Medea) killed my children,
Killed them,
Did not let me touch them,
Denied me the grace of burial.
I gave them life.
I saw them dead.
I curse you into eternity.

CHORUS: Zeus is a god who sees all from on high.
He gives and he takes.
What we expect,
He takes.
What we do not,
He gives.
Thus this story ends.

VIZ GRAPHIC NOVEL

INU-YASHA
A FEUDAL FAIRY TALE™
VOL. 1

STORY AND ART BY
RUMIKO TAKAHASHI

CONTENTS

SCROLL ONE
THE ACCURSED YOUTH

HOW... DARE YOU...

THE JEWEL...

FOR SUCH A THING...

LADY KIKYO...

WHAT TERRIBLE WOUNDS...

PLEASE, SISTER...

WE HAVE TO TAKE CARE OF YOU...

I WILL NOT LIVE.

LISTEN WELL, KAEDE...

TAKE THIS... AND *BURN* IT WITH MY REMAINS.

IT MUST NEVER...

...FALL INTO THE WRONG HANDS AGAIN!

TOKYO.
1997.

THE "SHIKON JEWEL"...?

FORTUNES
EXORCISMS
AMULETS/ WARDS
CONTACT GODS

fortunes ¥100   bear paws   talismans

YES.

SO LONG AS ONE HAS THIS, ONE'S FAMILY WILL KNOW SAFETY AND PROSPERITY.

AND PEOPLE ACTUALLY PAY MONEY...

...FOR THESE MARBLES?

SUNSET SHRINE

HEAR ITS LEGEND, KAGOME.

IN THE BEGINNING, THE "JEWEL OF FOUR SOULS"...

SUNSET SHRINE
Shikon Jewels

SUNSET SHRINE
Shikon Jewels

SAVE YOUR BREATH, GRAMPS.

YOU REMEMBER WHAT TOMORROW IS?

≈SIGH≈

COULD I EVER FOR- GET MY ADORABLE GRAND- DAUGHTER'S BIRTHDAY?

VIP

WOW! FOR ME?!

IT'S A DAY EARLY, BUT... HAPPY BIRTHDAY, KAGOME!

IT'S THE MUMMIFIED HAND OF A "KAPPA" WATER-SPRITE. THE LEGENDS HOLD THAT WHOSOEVER POSSESSES THIS...

HERE, BUYO. LUNCH.

DO YOU KNOW WHAT THOSE COST?!

MY "HOUSE" IS ALSO A VERY OLD SHRINE.

I LIVE WITH GRANDPA, MOM, AND MY LITTLE BROTHER.

THE LEGEND OF THESE PICKLES IS THAT...

YOU BOUGHT THEM FROM MR. UJIKO, RIGHT?

THERE'S A SACRED "GO-SHINBOKU" GOD-TREE THAT'S 500 YEARS OLD.

AND A COVERED WELL THAT PROBABLY HAS ITS OWN LEGEND.

IN FACT, EVERYTHING AT MY HOUSE HAS A LEGEND, BUT...

15

BUUU-YO!

KREEK...

HE'S SOME-WHERE DOWN THERE...

SO GO GET HIM OUT!

BUT DOESN'T THIS PLACE KINDA...GIVE YOU THE CREEPS...?

WHAT, YOU SCARED? YOU'RE A BOY, AREN'T YOU?

!

KCH KCH KCH

TH-THERE'S SOMETHING *IN* THERE!

LIKE, OH, SAY...OUR *CAT?!*

GASP

KCH KCH KCH

GEEZ...

HUH
?

KCH

KCH

KCH

IT'S COMING FROM... *INSIDE* THE WELL...?

YOU'RE KIDDING ME...

MIEW!!

PRR

PRR

YAAA !!

DON'T *YELL* LIKE THAT!! YOU *SCARED* ME!!

YOU LITTLE...

BA-BUMP BA-BUMP

!

KRIK...

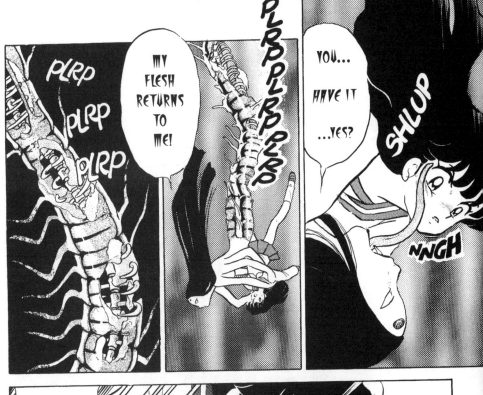

I...
WILL...
NOT...

...LOSE
IT
NOW...

...THE
JEWEL...

...OF
FOUR...

...SOULS...

JEWEL...
OF
FOUR...
?

I'M... IN THE WELL...?

SKUD

DNK
DNK
DNK

WAS THAT THING...

...JUST A DREAM...?

...GUESS NOT.

23

I WON'T LOSE IT NOW...

THE JEWEL OF FOUR SOULS...

"JEWEL OF FOUR SOULS"...

NOW WHAT DID GRAMPS SAY AGAIN...?

I... I'VE GOTTA GET OUT OF HERE...

SOTA! YOU *THERE*?!

GO GET GRAMPS! *NOW*!!

SKUT

CHICKEN... RUN AWAY, WILL HE...?

UFF.

HUH...?

HSSH...

I FELL INTO THE WELL INSIDE THE MINI-SHRINE... BUT...

WHERE'S THIS...?

GRAM-PA!!

MOM...?

ZASH ZASH

...NOW THERE WAS NO TRACE OF A SHRINE.

OH...!

THE OLD GOD-TREE...!

EVEN WHEN I WAS LITTLE, I COULD ALWAYS FIND MY WAY HOME FROM THERE...

ZASH ZASH

!!

A BOY...?

UM... ARE YOU OKAY...?

HELLO...?

hahh!

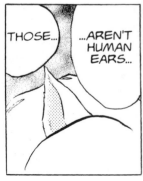
THOSE... ...AREN'T HUMAN EARS...

HSSH...

SUDDENLY... I WANT TO TOUCH THEM...

glp

SMF SMF SMF

...ALTHOUGH I KNOW IT'S NO TIME OR PLACE TO...

WHAT **DO** YOU THERE ?!

hyng

hyng

THIS LAND IS FORBID- DEN!

BE YOU A STRANGER ?!

...

YOU FOUND HER IN INU-YASHA'S FOREST...?

AYE, A LASS IN QUEEREST RAGS, SHE IS!

31

KIKYO WAS THE VILLAGE PRIESTESS...

AND ITS PROTECTRESS.

LISTEN WELL, KAEDE.

TAKE THIS... AND *BURN* IT WITH MY REMAINS.

THAT WAS OVER 50 YEARS AGO.

SHE DIED WHEN I WAS BUT A CHILD.

WHAT'S WRONG? NOT HUNGRY?

UM...

YOU THINK MAYBE YOU COULD *UNTIE* ME?

OH.

I... UH...

...DON'T S'POSE I'M IN TOKYO ANYMORE...?

I'VE NEVER HEARD THE NAME. IS THAT...

...THE LAND OF YOUR BIRTH?

I...UH... GUESS SO...

I WAS JUST THINKING THAT I SHOULD GET GOING SOON...

GOING...

BUT WHERE... AND HOW...?

WAAA!

BAKK BAKK BAKK.

WHAT COULD BE--?

BAM

AHH!

WHIIRN

WHOOOSH

NOR SPEARS NOR ARROWS STOP IT!

IF WE CAN LURE IT TO THE DRY OLD WELL, WE MIGHT TRAP IT!

DRY OLD WELL?!

IN INU-YASHA'S FOREST...

THE WELL I CRAWLED OUT OF...

WHERE'S THE FOREST?!

EAST, TOWARD...

TOWARD THAT LIGHT?! O--KAY...

YOU WILL NOT SLIP ME!

ZH ZH ZH ZH ZH ZH

THAT CHILD... DID SHE TRULY SAY...?

SHE SAW THE EVIL AURA OF THE FOREST...

THAT *NO* EARTHLY BEING CAN SEE!

hssh...

pirk!

D·KOOM

SCROLL TWO

INU-YASHA
RESURRECTED

WH-WHO ARE YOU...?

IT...HE... TALKED...

DESTROY HER WITH A SINGLE BLAST, KIKYO!

AFTER ALL...YOU DID IT TO ME.

"KIKYO"...?

WHOA, WHOA, WHOA! MY NAME'S...

SHE'S COMING.

ZAA!

WHAT...?

REALLY, KIKYO...I'M DISAPPOINTED...

LISTEN, YOU--

I DON'T KNOW WHO THIS "KIKYO" IS...

EXCEPT THAT SHE'S *NOT* ME!

FEH!

DO YOU EXPECT ME TO BELIEVE THAT I WOULDN'T KNOW THE *STENCH* OF THE GIRL WHO...

...HM?

HMM...

YOU'RE... *NOT* HER...!

GET IT NOW?

MY NAME'S KAGOME!

KA... GO... ME!

I'M A FOOL. AFTER ALL, KIKYO LOOKED INTELLIGENT...

AND PRETTY.

YOU...!

DNK DNK DNK

GBA

AAH...

LET... ME... GO!!

GYUUUUU

YOU LET ME GO!!

GROK

LADY KAEDE...

INU-YASHA...

!

INU-YASHA... IS AWAKE ?!

THAT SPELL WAS MEANT NEVER TO BREAK... BUT IT HAS!

HOW ?!

WHAT--
?!

SOME-
THING...
COME
OUT OF
HER...!

THE
JEWEL
OF
FOUR
SOULS--
!!

!

UH...

top...

KOR-
ROR-
ROP...

IT WAS... INSIDE OF ME...?

ZZZZAAA

I KNEW, I KNEW, I KNEW YOU WERE HIDING IT!

THAT JEWEL IS *MINE!!*

WHAT...?

GIVE IT TO ME!

ZH!
ZH!

!

domp-

HEH
HEH
HEH
HEH...

"INU-YASHA WHO SEEKS THE SHIKON JEWEL..." I HAVE HEARD OF A HALF-DEMON BY SUCH A NAME...

AT LAST WE MEET...

53

I'M GOING TO DIE HERE... CRUSHED BY A...

MSH

MSH

MSH

UNKH

MSH

HEY.

THIS ARROW.

CAN YOU PULL IT OUT?

WHAT...?!

NNGG...

YOU MUST *NOT* !!

THAT ARROW CONTAINS THE SPELL!

YOU MUST NOT SET HIM FREE!

AND WHAT DO YOU WANT, WITCH?!

TO BECOME A CENTIPEDE'S DESSERT?!

ONCE HER BODY HAS DIGESTED THE JEWEL OF FOUR SOULS...

...NONE OF US WILL BE ABLE TO STOP HER!

SSHH SSHH

WELL, GIRL?!!

DO YOU WANT TO DIE HERE WITH ME?!

GNSH GNSH

NO...I WON'T DIE...NOT IN THIS...

...STINKING HELL!

gyn

LIVE AGAIN, INU-YASHA!!

GZA

BAKKL BAKKL

DOM

BRROP
BRROP

I HAD... NO IDEA...

HE WAS SO POWERFUL...

60

YOU GOTTA BE KIDDING... IT'S STILL MOVING...?

ZHA-WA

ZHA-WA ZHA-WA

CAN YOU SEE A PLACE WHERE THE FLESH GLOWS?!

THE SHIKON JEWEL MUST BE BURNING INSIDE HER!

BUT...

UNLESS YOU REMOVE THE JEWEL, HER BODY WILL RESURRECT ITSELF THROUGH TIME WITHOUT END!

WHADDYA MEAN...

...UNLESS I REMOVE IT?!

ZHA-WA

ZHWA ZHWA

WAIT! I SEE IT!!

POHH...

YOU'RE TELLING ME...THAT THIS "JEWEL OF FOUR SOULS" THING-A-MA-JIG...

...GIVES POWER TO DEMONS...?

EXACTLY.

MEANING THERE'S NO POINT IN A MORTAL KEEPING IT.

SO BE A GOOD LITTLE GIRL AND HAND IT OVER...

...UNLESS YOU'D RATHER FEEL THE CARESS OF MY CLAWS!

SHAAA...

WHAT...?

SCROLL THREE
A NEW FOE

64

DO YOU THINK I'M TOO GENTLE, LITTLE GIRL?

gik-kik...

NOT WHEN...

...YOU *STINK* OF THE WOMAN WHO *KILLED* ME!!

YEEE!!

ZAH

OOWAH!

BRRA BRRA

NEXT TIME... I'LL CUT YOU IN HALF...

SHHHUU

EENNN

HEY!

YOU'RE REALLY TRYING TO *HURT* ME, AREN'T YOU?!

LADY KAEDE, ME-THINKS...

...WE'D HAVE PREFERRED THE GIANT CENTIPEDE AFTER ALL!

SIGH... OH, ME...

'TIS EVER THUS.

ZHARA

I AM RINGED BY FOOLS...

KAGOME!

UTTER A SUBDUING SPELL!

A SUB--?

WHA--?!

IT MATTERS NOT WHICH!

ANY WORD TO SUBDUE HIM!

OH--OH--OH, NO...

BUT...

BUT I DON'T *KNOW* ANY...!

YOU...

...SUBDUE ME?!

DOKKA

DON'T MAKE ME LAUGH!

BHA

UH...

UH...

70

BUT WHAT A PLACE WE'RE LEFT IN, EH?

NOW THAT THE SHIKON JEWEL HAS APPEARED AGAIN IN THIS WORLD...

O W W W

HERE, LET ME SEE THAT WOUND.

SOME HEALING HERBS SHOULD TAKE CARE OF IT...

...THE EVIL BEINGS WHO DESIRE ITS POWER WILL SOON BE FLOCKING HERE.

UM...YOU MEAN... LIKE MONSTERS...?

NOT *ONLY* MONSTERS.

BUT ALSO MEN... WHO ARE SOMETIMES WORSE...

YOU...WHY DO *YOU* WANT THE JEWEL?

...

IN THIS ERA OF WAR AND CHAOS, THE POWERS OF THE JEWEL OF FOUR SOULS...

...CAN MAKE ANY AMBITION A REALITY.

BRRR...

YOU'RE STRONG.

WHY DO YOU NEED MORE POWER?

HE'S ONLY HALF A DEMON...

HO...

IS THAT SO....?

THE LITTLE WITCH KICKED IT, EH?

WELL.

heh

NICE TO HEAR SOME GOOD NEWS.

INU-YASHA...

POP

I WOULDN'T START CELEBRATING JUST YET.

THERE IS THE MATTER OF REINCARNATION. DON'T YOU AGREE... KAGOME?

UH...

YOUR OUTWARD LIKENESS. YOUR MYSTIC ABILITIES.

AND THE SHIKON JEWEL HIDDEN WITHIN YOUR BODY. WHAT OTHER ANSWER IS THERE?

YOU WERE BORN TO PROTECT THAT JEWEL.

YOU GOTTA BE KIDDING...

RI-
RI-
RI-

IT'S BEEN TWO DAYS...

...SINCE I CAME HERE.

MOM...

GRANDPA...

SOTA...

THEY MUST BE SO WORRIED.

I...I HAVE TO...

...FIND A WAY HOME...

HSH...

THERE'S THE FIRST OF THEM, SNIFFING OUT THE SCENT OF THE JEWEL...

WHP...

CROW-DEMON...

THAT MEANS TROUBLE...

SHAWA

THE DRY WELL IN INU-YASHA'S FOREST...

BOY

THAT'S WHERE I CAME OUT.

SO MAY-BE...

...THE WAY HOME IS THERE.

HYOOOOOO...

A GIRL...

GIRL...

THOOK

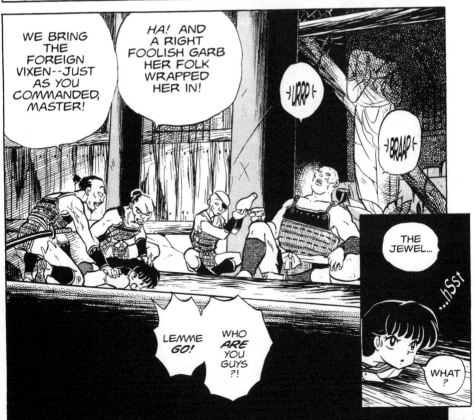

WE BRING THE FOREIGN VIXEN--JUST AS YOU COMMANDED, MASTER!

HA! AND A RIGHT FOOLISH GARB HER FOLK WRAPPED HER IN!

-URRP-

-BRAAP-

THE JEWEL...

...hSSt

LEMME GO!

WHO *ARE* YOU GUYS?!

WHAT?

-URP!-

OH...
!

NOT **ONLY**
MONSTERS.

BUT ALSO
MEN...
WHO ARE
SOMETIMES
WORSE.

NO
!!

GIVE
IT--
!

90

INU-
YASHA...

WHAT...?!

WHO WOULD DARE...?!

YOU... YOU CAME TO SAVE...

WHERE'S THE SHIKON JEWEL?!

...TO SAVE... ME...?

THE JEWEL!!

→YMRP→

→RAAP→

SHH!!

SO... HERE YOU ARE...

shhh...

WHAT A VILE SCENT.

THE SCENT... OF A HALF-DECAYED *CORPSE*!

HUH...?

SHREE! SHREE! SHREE!

UHH...

HYA-AAA-AHH!!

GASP!

EEEEEEEE!!

BEEN EATING *CHEST* ALL NIGHT, EH...

...TO MAKE YOURSELF A COZY LITTLE NEST?

THE MASTER... HE'S DEAD...?

I *THOUGHT* HE WAS ACTIN' A MITE STRANGE...

THAT'S SO... *SICK*...

CAW CAW CAW

TOO WEAK TO FIGHT YOUR OWN BATTLES...

...OR EVEN TO MANIPULATE THE LIVING, EH?!

BRAWD

GNCHH

VOOON

SHA

I WON'T LET YOU!

GNN

STOP, YOU COWARD!!

HYU

COME!

GWIH

WHA...

101

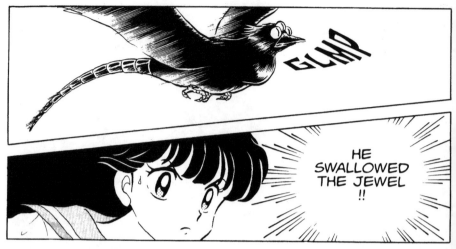

GLMP

HE SWALLOWED THE JEWEL !!

FLY **STEADY** !!

I WILL.

HMPH.

ONCE SHE'S SHOT THAT CROW--I'LL HAVE NO MORE NEED OF **HER**...

...AND THE GROUND IS A LONG WAY DOWN!

ONE **SHOT**, GIRL!

KIKYO WAS A **MASTER** OF THE BOW!

I TOLD YOU, I'M **KAGOME**!

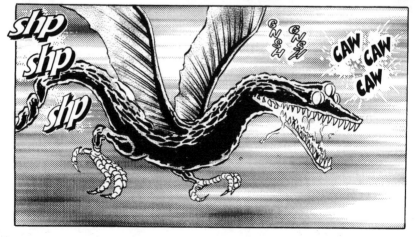

SCROLL FIVE
KAGOME'S ARROW

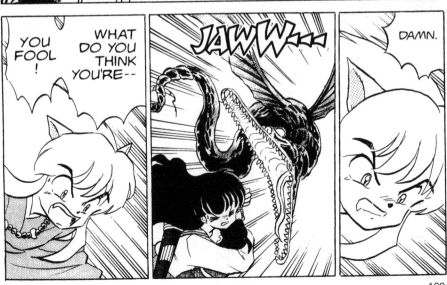

FWAPP FWAPP

I SEE IT!

UNDER ITS WING!

bwop

KRIK KROK

CURSE THE THING!

IT'LL GO ON FLYING---- UNTIL ITS HELL-BORN CORPSE ABSORBS THE WHOLE BLASTED *JEWEL*!

!

I'VE GOT TO DO SOMETHING... *FAST!* BUT...

OH.

SHWIP

TUGG

KRIK
KRIK
KRIK

WHAT...

THIS TIME...

SHOOTIN' FROM SO FAR OFF...

YOU DON'T HAVE A CHANCE, GIRL.

NOT AS FEEBLE WITH THE BOW AS *YOU* ARE...

IF THIS SHIKON JEWEL MAKES HIM RE-GENERATE...

...THEN THE LEG'S GOT TO HEAD BACK TO THE REST OF THE BODY... RIGHT?

GWMM...

DOOSH

PANNG

SHE... SHE STRUCK IT!

YES!!

115

LADY KAEDE... TH-THAT LIGHT...!

!

THIS...

...DOES NOT BODE WELL...

SOMETHING ABOUT THAT FLASH...

...CHILLS ME TO THE BONE...

ZHK ZHK

ARE YOU SURE THE JEWEL'S THIS WAY, FOOL?!

I...I JUST HAVE THIS *FEELING* THAT...

EH ?!

FWAP

KRR.RAK.

FWAP FWAP FWAP

SO QUICKLY ?!

CAW CAW CAW

SHHHH

JUST ITS... HEAD ?!

HEH.

AT LAST WE GO HEAD TO HEAD, EH ?!

BRAK

DIE, DEMON!!

BOSH

GLINT...

WHAT...?

THE JEWEL--

UM...

I GUESS IT *COULD* BE...

A LITTLE *PIECE*...

OF THE JEWEL...

NO...

HOW CAN THIS *BE*?!

QUIT HOWLING, INU-YASHA.

THE *JEWEL*! WHAT HAPPENED TO THE BLASTED *JEWEL*?!

WHEN KAGOME SHOT HER MAGIC ARROW...

...IT SHATTERED NOT ONLY THE DEMON, BUT THE JEWEL OF FOUR SOULS WITHIN IT.

IT MIGHT HAVE SPLIT INTO TEN PIECES, OR INTO A HUNDRED...

...BUT NOW THEY ARE SCATTERED EVERY-WHERE.

IF A SINGLE SLIVER SHOULD FALL INTO THE HANDS OF AN EVIL SPIRIT...

THE RESULT MIGHT BE AS ILL AS IF THAT SPIRIT HAD DEVOURED THE ENTIRE JEWEL!

AND IT'S ALL... MY FAULT...?

121

LISTEN, THEN.

KAGOME... INU-YASHA...

YOU MUST GATHER THE SHARDS OF THE SHIKON JEWEL AND RESTORE IT TO ITS ORIGINAL FORM. *TOGETHER.*

YOU MEAN...?

HA.

ARE YOU SURE, KAEDE?

I'M ONE OF THOSE "EVIL SPIRITS" AFTER THE JEWEL, REMEMBER?

FOR NOW... THERE'S NO OTHER CHOICE.

BUT... BUT ALL I WANT...

IS TO *GO HOME* !

SCROLL SIX
YURA OF THE HAIR

NO WAY!

I'M COVERED IN BLOOD 'N' MUD 'N' **DEMON-SLIME**...

...AND I CAN'T STAND IT ANY MORE!

MAN. I DIDN'T EVEN THINK THERE **WAS** A TIME...

...BEFORE HOT BATHS!

HSH SH...

IS IT SO? THAT LADY KAGOME'S UNDERGOIN' THE SACRED WATER RITE?

FOR PURIFICATION, IT MUST BE! FOR NEW MAGIC POWERS!

THEY SAY IF A MAN SPIES ON SUCH A RITE... HE'LL BE PUNISHED BY THE GODS!

HSH. HSH...

...

KAGOME...

INU-YASHA...

YOU MUST GATHER THE SHARDS OF THE SHIKON JEWEL AND RESTORE IT TO ITS ORIGINAL FORM. *TOGETHER.*

BUT I DON'T EVEN KNOW *HOW*...

...AND INU-YASHA'S LIKE AN ANIMAL...

SPLSH...

SIT, BOY !!

BLASH!

GAAH!!

SO... SEE ANY-THING GOOD?

HOW COULD I FORGET... THE WENCH'S NECK-LACE AND ITS WORD-SPELLS?!

I KNEW YOU WERE AN *ANIMAL*, BUT... BUT *THIS*...!

FEH. YOU'RE AS STUPID AS YOU ARE VAIN.

I WAS ONLY-----

--LOOKING FOR A CHANCE TO STEAL THE SHIKON JEWEL SHARD, IS THAT IT?

HMPH. SEEMS AT LEAST *YOU* HAVE A BRAIN IN YOUR WITHERED HEAD.

WHAT...?

NO. YOU'RE JUST TOO PREDICTABLE... →SIGH←

127

HEY.

HEY, WHAT.

BWAT BWAT

TAKE OFF THOSE CLOTHES.

GONNNNG

WHAT... WAS *THAT* FOR...?

YOU'RE AN ANIMAL.

ZZZ

I DIDN'T SAY "GET NAKED"!

JUST GET BACK INTO YOUR OWN WEIRD CLOTHES!

BECAUSE THESE MAKE ME LOOK LIKE KIKYO?!

BWAT BWAT

THAT HAS NOTHING TO DO WITH IT.

feh

IS HE A DEMON OR A JUNIOR-HIGH KID?!

130

YOU KNOW, IF YOU CAN'T BE A LITTLE MORE CIVILIZED...

...WE'RE NEVER GONNA BE ABLE TO WORK TOGETHER.

THAT'D BE FINE WITH ME.

I'LL FIND THOSE SHARDS EVEN IF I HAVE TO DO IT ALONE.

HMF.

OH, REALLY.

THEN YOU DON'T NEED ME AROUND, HUH?

WHAT...?

WHERE ARE YOU GOING?

I'VE MADE UP MY MIND.

FLAP FLAP

I'M GOING HOME.

'BYE, ANIMAL! IT'S BEEN REAL!

"HOME"...?

WAIT!!

UH-UH.

IT'S NO USE TRYING TO STOP ME.

BUT YOU HAVE A SHARD OF THE JEWEL!

LEAVE IT HERE!

YOU MEAN THIS?

SIT!!

WHY-Y-Y, YOU...

MOOSH...

FLAP FLAP

LATER, DUDE!

HYUUUUU

THIS WAY, LADY KAEDE.

SHE WAS HALE AND HEALTHY THIS MORNING, BUT...

LET ME LOOK...

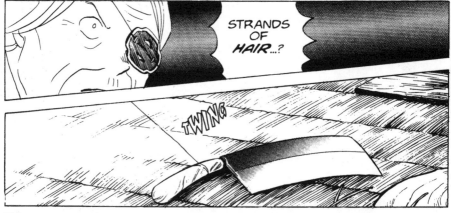

WSH

SNOOWOOE

HAAAA

SPAT

EEEEE!

hssh...

THE DRY WELL I CLIMBED OUT OF!

IF THERE'S ANY WAY TO GET HOME, IT'S HERE...

GULP

BONES...
?

THEY CALL IT THE "BONE-EATER'S WELL."

IT IS A DUMPING GROUND FOR THE CORPSES OF DEMONS AND MONSTERS.

PASS BY A FEW DAYS LATER... AND THE CORPSES WILL HAVE VANISHED.

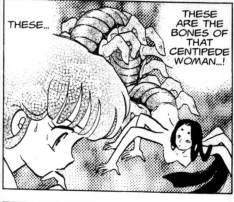

THESE...

THESE ARE THE BONES OF THAT CENTIPEDE WOMAN...!

NO...
NO...

I CAN'T GO IN THERE...

YURA OF THE HAIR.

BUT I WON'T BE OFFENDED IF YOU DON'T REMEMBER IT.

FOR YOUR LIFE IS ABOUT TO END.

ZAH

BR BR BR

VII!

PNG

PNG

OH...!

SVOOP

142

LA--
?

SHE'S...
GONE...
?

...

WHO...
WAS
THAT
GIRL?

I'M
GOING
HOME.

FARE-
WELL,
INU-
YASHA.

ZOP

FEH.

GOOD RIDDANCE.

WITH HER GONE, I FEEL LIKE I'VE HAD A *LEASH* TAKEN OFF!

NH ?!

ZZZZZZZ

SNOOT

SNOOT

WHY ARE YOUR WOMEN AFTER *ME?*

THEY ARE ALL UNDER THE POWER OF SOMEONE... OR SOME*THING*... ELSE.

WHERE IS KAGOME?

CALL KAGOME AND BRING HER HERE!

NO NEED. I CAN TAKE CARE OF THIS MYSELF, HAG!

NO! NO, YOU MUST NOT...!

THIS TIME, WITH THIS OPPONENT...

...WE *NEED* KAGOME!

WELL, THIS TIME...

...I REALLY *MUST* GET THE NECK!

GWI-I-P

CURSE IT...

BI-I-NG

BAKK BAKK

THIS SLACK...

LA?

THE FLESH HAS *NOT* BEEN SEVERED...?

I LOOKED DEATH IN THE EYE FOR A MOMENT THERE...

A MERE *HUMAN* WOULD BE HEADLESS NOW.

HUHH HUHH

WOBBLE...

ZWAH...

!

TSK, A NEW CREW.

WE WON'T MAKE ANY PROGRESS AT THIS RATE, OLD CRONE!

154

WHERE AM I...?

SHF...

OH YEAH...

THAT GIRL CHASED ME...

IT IS NO USE TRYING TO ESCAPE!

...AND I FELL INTO...

BUT WE'VE ALREADY *LOOKED* IN THE WELL!

I SAW HER FALL IN, *REALLY*!

YOU MUST'VE BEEN DREAMING...

TAKK

BUT GRAMPA, I *SAW* IT!

GR-GRAM-*PAA*!

SO-*TAA*!!

THE
BUILDINGS...

FORTUNES
EXORCISMS
AMULETS/
WARDS
CONTACT
GODS

I'M...

HOME...
?!

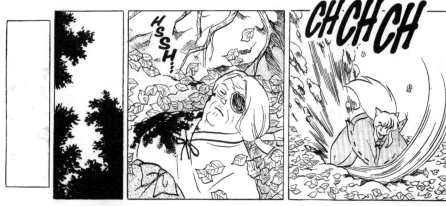

HSSH!!

CH CH CH

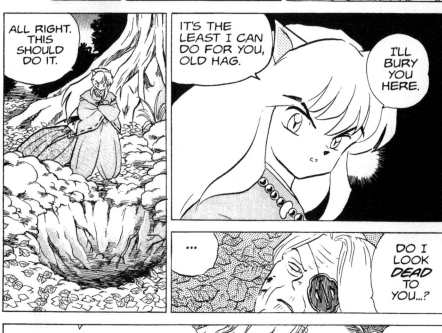

ALL RIGHT. THIS SHOULD DO IT.

IT'S THE LEAST I CAN DO FOR YOU, OLD HAG.

I'LL BURY YOU HERE.

...

DO I LOOK *DEAD* TO YOU...?

I'M SAYING, *HIDE* HERE!

I'LL COME BACK FOR YOU LATER... IF I DON'T FORGET.

VSH VSH

SEE THAT YOU DO NOT, BOY!

hsh hsh hsh

CURSE THAT GIRL...

WHERE IS SHE NOW THAT I FINALLY *WANT* HER?!

SsSS

AAH....

I'M NOT HOME... I'M IN HEAVEN...

...

BUT, FATHER... KAGOME'S STORY...COULD IT BE TRUE...?

C'MON, GRAMPS, YOU KNOW IT IS!

A MONSTER CAME OUTTA THE WELL AND GRABBED HER AN'...

THE LEGEND HAS BEEN PASSED DOWN THROUGH THE AGES ABOUT "THE BONE-EATER'S WELL"...

TELLING OF AN EVIL WITHIN IT THAT CAUSES THE CORPSES OF MONSTERS TO DISAPPEAR... SOMEWHERE...

WHAT IF THAT "SOMEWHERE" WERE THE STREAM OF TIME...?

I CAN'T JUST *SIT* HERE!

TNG TNG TNG

ALL RIGHT.

HUH... SPELLS?

YUP.

162

I SEALED IT WITH NEW, WONDER-WORKING SPELL-SCROLLS AND SET UP A WARDING SHIELD.

THAT WELL WILL REMAIN SHUT FOREVER!

SOME-HOW...

...EVERY-THING THAT HAPPENED SEEMS LIKE A DREAM...

...BUT STILL...

I CAN'T HELP WONDERING...

...IF EVERYTHING IS ALL RIGHT IN *THAT* WORLD.

NO MISTAKE. IT'S HER SCENT...

Snf Snf Snf

IT'S THAT GIRL'S CLOTHES...

SO SHE ESCAPED DOWN *HERE* !

...

Snf Snf Snf

"THAT WELL WILL REMAIN SHUT FOREVER!"

SCROLL EIGHT
THE RETURN HOME

OH, *MY*!

JUST LOOK WHAT YOU'VE DONE TO THE SHIKON JEWEL!

THAT YURA OF THE HAIR...WAS THAT WHAT SHE CALLED HERSELF?...

I WONDER WHO SHE WAS...

OR WHAT SHE WAS...

WHEN HE FINDS OUT SHE TOOK THE SLIVER OF THE JEWEL FROM ME...

I'LL BET INU-YASHA WILL WANT TO KILL ME...

LEAVING? THAT'D BE FINE WITH ME.

I'LL FIND THOSE SHARDS... ALONE!

YEAH, RIGHT...

INU-YASHA DOESN'T NEED *ME* AROUND...

167

STOP IT!

SMAT

I'M GONNA FORGET EVERYTHING THAT HAPPENED!

AFTER ALL... I'M NEVER GOING BACK *THERE* AGAIN!

HYUuuuu

HEY GRAMPS...

grble bbl

...Y'KNOW THE SPELLS YOU PUT ON THE WELL...

WHO TOLD YOU THAT YOU COULD COME TROTTING HOME, EH...?!

YOU...

B-BUT HOW...

WHERE... WHERE DID YOU...?

THE WELL, FOOL! WHERE ELSE?!

THE WELL?

BUT...

IT'S A LIE!

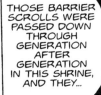

THOSE BARRIER SCROLLS WERE PASSED DOWN THROUGH GENERATION AFTER GENERATION IN THIS SHRINE, AND THEY...

SCROLLS? YOU MEAN THESE SCRAPS OF PAPER?

YOU THOUGHT THEY COULD STOP *ME*?

AW, GEE, GRAMPS...

PRAA

gasp

HEY! WAIT!

WHAT'RE YOU...?

COME ON, LET'S GO!

gnng

171

172

WHAT HAIR?

YOU... CAN'T YOU SEE IT?!

TWK

OH...!

CHK

IT'S MOVING!

TK...

KAGOME, YOU'RE BLEEDING...

WHAT'S WRONG?!

I'M THE ONLY ONE WHO CAN SEE IT...

IS THIS SOME OF YURA'S HAIR...?!

IT CAN'T BE...

WELL, KAEDE-HAG WAS RIGHT.

YOUR EYES WORK WELL ENOUGH.

YOU... IDIOT...

HOW DARE YOU BRING SUCH A HORRIBLE THING WITH YOU!

KAGOME!

WHAT'S GOIN' ON...?

STAY OUT! YOU MUSTN'T COME IN!

CRRRAAK

BMM

HERE...

I'VE GOT TO STOP IT HERE...

FWAA

KAGOME!

OPEN THE DOOR, KAGOME!!

BLAST IT!

RRP RRP

ffSSHH

SHSHSHSH

ZWRR

DM DM

IF YOU CUT THEM, STILL MORE COME OUT TO TAKE THEIR PLACE...

THERE'S NO END TO IT...

AGH!

HSSHH

177

OH...!

ELNT...

THAT'S IT!!

VSH

THAT'S THE STRAND THAT'S MANIPULATING THE REST OF THE HAIR!

INU-YASHA, THIS ONE!

CUT *THIS* STRAND!

HERE?!

HWSS

IF HE CAN'T SEE IT, HE'LL NEVER...

WAIT... I KNOW...

IT'S GONE...

THAT'S FUNNY...

IF ALL YURA OF THE HAIR WANTS IS THE SHIKON JEWEL...

THEN WHY IS SHE STILL AFTER INU-YASHA?

IS HE HER REAL TARGET? OR AM I?!

INU-YASHA!

WE'RE GOING BACK!!

WHY? A MOMENT AGO YOU WERE RUNNING AWAY FROM THIS WAR.

BUT YOU WOULDN'T **LET** ME, WOULD YOU?!

IF I STAY IN THE PRESENT...

...MY WHOLE FAMILY MIGHT BE DRAGGED INTO THIS TOO!

FWFF

IT'S CLOTH SPUN FROM THE FUR OF A FIRE RAT.

IT'S STRONGER THAN ANY SUIT OF ARMOR.

TH-THANKS...

YOU'LL NEED IT...WITH SKIN AS WEAK AND FRAIL AS YOURS.

YOU ALWAYS KNOW JUST WHAT TO SAY.

TO BE CONTINUED...